The ABC Mystery

Story and Pictures by
Doug Cushman

HarperCollins*Publishers*

The ABC Mystery
Copyright © 1993 by Doug Cushman
Printed in the U.S.A. All rights reserved.
Typography by Daniel C. O'Leary
2   3   4   5   6   7   8   9   10
❖

Library of Congress Cataloging-in-Publication Data
Cushman, Doug.
    The ABC mystery / story and pictures by Doug Cushman.
        p.   cm.
    Summary: An alphabetical list of people, objects, and clues leads Inspector
McGroom to a stolen work of art.
    ISBN 0-06-021226-8. — ISBN 0-06-021227-6 (lib. bdg.)
    [1. Mystery and detective stories.   2. Alphabet.   3. Stories in rhyme.]
I. Title.
PZ8.3.C96Ab   1993   92-9621
[E]—dc20   CIP
                                                                        AC

For Nancy, who loves a good mystery

A is the **A**rt that was stolen at night.

B is the **B**utler, who sneaks out of sight.

C is the **C**lue that's left in the room.

D is **D**etective Inspector McGroom.

E is the **E**ye that looks through the glass.

F is the **F**ootprint that's found in the grass.

G is the **G**ardener, who saw nothing that day.

H is his **H**elper, who has nothing to say.

I is **I**nspector, who ponders the case.

J is **J**alopy, in which they give chase.

K is the **K**ilt that the bagpiper wore.

L is the **L**ake with a boat on the shore.

M is the **M**anor that stands on the moor.

N is the **N**umber of steps to the door.

O is the **O**rgan that sounds in the hall.

P is the **P**ainting with eyes that see all.

Q is the **Query** Dame Agatha makes.

R is the **R**obber, who's seen by mistake.

S is the **S**tairs to the cellar below.

T is the **T**unnel through which they must go.

U is **U**mbrella that pries the door wide.

V is the **V**ault with the artwork inside.

W is **W**ombat and a den full of thieves.

X is the kiss the Inspector receives.

Y is a **Y**awn with the red setting sun.

$\mathbb{Z}$ is asleep . . . and a job that's well done.